The Faith Puzzle

SUSIE GUILL

THE FAITH PUZZLE

Copyright 2025 by Susan Guill
All rights reserved

No part of this work may be reproduced or transmitted in any form or by any means, electronic or mechanical, including photocopying and recording, or by any information storage or retrieval system, except as may be expressly permitted by the 1976 Copyright Act or in writing from the publisher. Requests for permission can be addressed to Inscript Books, a division of Dove Christian Publishers, P.O. Box 611, Bladensburg, MD 20710-0611, www.inscriptpublishing.com.

Paperback ISBN 978-1-957497-74-7

Inscript and the portrayal of a pen with script are trademarks of Dove Christian Publishers.

Published in the United States of America

Scripture quotations are from the ESV® Bible (The Holy Bible, English Standard Version®), © 2001 by Crossway, a publishing ministry of Good News Publishers. ESV Text Edition: 2025. The ESV text may not be quoted in any publication made available to the public by a Creative Commons license. The ESV may not be translated in whole or in part into any other language. Used by permission. All rights reserved.

THE FAITH PUZZLE

Chapter 1

Faith Stockwell was born and raised in a small farming town in South Texas. You know the kind: everyone knows your name, and everyone knows your business; yep, that's the one. It's the kind of town where you never feel alone and, at the same time, you can never really be alone. Most of the people in Millstone are kind, helpful, and always willing to lend a hand whenever needed. Generations of Millstone families have grown up together and still remain close. Yes, several youths have gone off to college after graduation, never to return, but others stayed in Millstone to become farmers, just like their fathers and grandfathers before them. A few stayed out of obligation to their families, but most stayed because they love the land, the town, and the people who live there. Faith was one of the ones who got married, moved to Chicago, and only visited during holidays and summers. But she's back in Millstone now, probably for good.

It's early morning, and Faith places Lily, her basset hound, in the passenger seat of an old, sunbeaten, red farm pickup truck. Lily is proudly wearing a brown cowboy hat, excitedly wagging her tail, certain that she is going into town. Faith starts the truck and begins the fifteen-minute drive to the Millstone Town Hall building. She leans over and turns on a CD of Hanson's *MMMBop*. Faith looks over at Lily and chuckles. "Here's your jam, Lily." Lily wags her tail as she looks at Faith, seeming to like the song. They drive all the way to town from Faith's farm listening to music.

When they arrive, Faith parks the truck directly in front of the town hall office. She gets a bright red Radio Flyer wagon from the bed of the truck and places Lily in it. She walks through town, heading to the post office as she pulls Lily in the wagon. As she enters the post office, she greets Bea, the sweet, friendly postmaster in her late seventies, loved by everyone in Millstone.

"Morning, Bea".

"Morning, Faith. Morning, Councilwoman Lily".

"Ha, ha, very funny, Bea."

Bea looks down at Lily with a confused expression. "Is it Wednesday already?"

Faith replies as she rolls her eyes, "No, it's still Tuesday. I was in a hurry and put the wrong hat on her this morning. Why my mother put hats on this dog is beyond me. And what's worse, she designated a different hat for each day of the week."

Bea sorts through the mail as she responds. "Oh, your mother thought it was funny dressing up Lily, and the whole town got a kick out of it. Besides, it helps me remember what day it is. The real prize was putting Lily's name on the town council ballot. In her wildest dreams, she never thought that pooch would win." Bea chuckles. "Your mama had an incredible sense of humor, and everyone loved her. And honestly, that dog's an asset to the town council." Bea chuckles again.

Faith glances at her wristwatch. "Well, I've got about twenty minutes to get her to the council meeting. We don't want to be late. The mayor hates tardiness, but he really loves this dog almost as much as I do."

Bea turns towards Faith. "How does she vote anyway?"

"One bark for yes and two barks for no, and no bark is undecided. She was the deciding vote for the new playground equipment at the park." Faith says as she laughs. "She's actually doing a decent job. Any mail, Bea?"

"Well, yes." Bea hands Faith her mail as she discloses what's in a letter. "Ben, your long-lost little brother, will be down in a few weeks to help you go through your parents' things."

"It's about time. I mean, it's been three months since the accident," Faith says as she reaches for the letter.

Bea smirks as she says, "And he's bringing his new girlfriend to meet you."

Faith takes the letter. "Another one?"

Bea beams as she replies, "He's proposing to this one."

Faith opens the letter quickly to read what her brother wrote.

"Really? Well, it's about time for that, too."

As Faith reads through the letter, Pastor Sam Wright, a man in his fifties and strikingly good-looking, walks in.

"Is it Wednesday already?" Sam says as he looks down at Lily.

Faith sneers at Sam. "I put the wrong hat on her this morning." Faith looks back down and continues to read the letter from her brother.

Sam laughs and turns his attention towards Bea. "Any mail, Bea?

"Yes, your niece is pregnant again." Bea warmly hands Sam his mail.

Faith looks up from the letter towards Sam. "Another baby? Wow, what's that like? Twelve?"

Sam replies with a matter-of-fact tone, "No, it's their fourth."

Faith smiles and returns to reading her brother's letter, saying, "She pops babies out like a Pez machine pops out candy."

Bea cannot help but laugh at Faith's remark, but Sam remains unfazed, "Well, she and her husband want a big family."

Bea decides to voice her opinion. "People just don't have big families anymore. Glad to hear it."

Sam seems pleased with Bea's support. "Well, they can afford a big family, so I'm happy for them. Speaking of family, how's Cricket?"

Faith puts her brother's letter in her pocket. "She's doing really well, super busy. You know, the CEO of her own magazine keeps her running seven days a week. I miss her, but I'm really proud of my daughter and all that she's accomplished."

Sam looks concerned. "Is she coming to visit any-time soon?"

Faith takes a breath and sighs, "I doubt it. She travels all over interviewing bands for the music section of the magazine. I think she's in Vegas this week. She calls to check on me, but we don't get into lengthy conversa-tions."

Sam seems shocked at her answer. "You're kidding, right? You two were so close."

"We're still close; she's just so busy. And since her dad died, she really sinks herself into her work. They weren't close, and I know it bothers her that they never had the connection that she and I do. He worked all the time and never seemed to make time for her. He missed every concert, play, game, all her school events. He barely made it to her college graduation. She never got over it." Faith looks down at her watch.

Bea feels the need to say something positive. "Well, then, he missed out because she is a lovely girl. We're so proud of her."

Faith smiles tenderly at Bea. "I just don't want her to work her life away like her dad did, all those wasted years."

Sam responds with encouragement. "She won't. She's a sweet and intelligent girl. You did a good job raising her. Trust and give her time."

Faith looks back at her wristwatch. "That's all I got is time. Wow, speaking of time, I've got to run and get Lily to the town council meeting, or she will be late. Bye, Bea. Bye, Sam."

"Bye, Hun. Bye, Councilwoman," Bea says, giggling again at the thought of Lily being on the town council.

Sam remembers his and Faith's dinner plans and yells, "Don't forget dinner at Dad's at seven sharp!"

Sam sees Faith raise her hand to show she heard him.

Just as Faith leaves the post office and begins her

walk to the city council meeting, she starts thinking to herself. Faith just didn't understand why Sam chose to be a minister. Sam was the high school quarterback, voted most likely to succeed, and had an academic scholarship to any college of his choosing. He was the best-looking guy in high school, and in town, for that matter. He had, and still has, that smoldering Kevin Sorbo look about him. All the girls would swoon when he walked down the school hallways, but he never seemed to care. He was smart, funny, and Faith's absolute best friend. Sam and Faith lived about two miles apart and have been best friends since kindergarten. He had the world at his fingertips and would have been successful at anything he chose to do. He gave all that up to become a minister. Faith just couldn't get past the feeling that he was missing out on life. But Faith loved Sam and would support him in anything he chose to do, even becoming a minister.

Faith breathes heavily. "We made it."

Faith and Lily enter the council meeting. She places Lily beside the mayor at the council table. Mayor Talbert leans over to Lily and gives her a jelly donut and pats her head. Faith rolls her eyes and sits on the other side of Lily at the table.

Mayor Talbert places his notes on the table and says, "Okay, everyone is here. Let's get started."

***

Sam is still talking to Bea at the post office when a new resident enters. She is dressed in a beige designer business suit and introduces herself to Bea.

"Hello. I'm Sandra Simmons."

Bea replies with a hint of excitement, "Oh, you must be Randy Simmons' new wife. So glad to finally meet you. You know, we were excited when we heard Randy was moving back to town after he graduated from college. His folks are so proud that he decided to practice medicine here in Millstone. Oh, I mean Dr. Simmons. We are so proud of him. I used to babysit him and change his diapers when he was a baby. Such a good boy." Bea smiles at Sandra.

Sandra, not impressed with the small-town talk, gives no expression to Bea. "Well, Randy asked me to come in and check for any mail."

Bea hands Sandra the mail and then immediately starts to tell Sandra what is in one of the letters. "Well, your sister is coming to visit this Friday, and your dad is thinking about selling the boathouse in Maine."

Sandra, standing with a look of shock and irritation on her face, scolds Bea, "Did you read my mail?"

"Oh, well, yes, just the letter."

Sandra, still in disbelief that her mail was read, raises her voice at Bea. "You are aware that it's illegal to read someone else's mail! Especially by the postmaster."

Bea quietly responds, realizing that Sandra is upset. "Well, it's not illegal in Millstone. It's our town tradition. Oh, I see Randy didn't mention this to you." Bea looks at Sandra with a sorrowful look.

"No, he forgot to mention it to me, but I'm sure going to mention it to him when I get home this evening." Sandra turns to go, giving Bea a determined look. Sam follows Sandra out the door, hoping to mend the situation.

Sam catches up to Sandra. "Mrs. Simmons, please wait."

Sandra turns around with an impatient look on her face.

"I'm Sam Wright, a minister here in Millstone. Bea means well. And reading the mail *is* a tradition here in Millstone. Believe it or not, the townspeople really enjoy it. It's part of our history and we are very proud of it."

Sandra sneers at Sam. "Your history? Really?"

"Yes, look, when the town was first founded in 1850, no one could read except for Mr. Millstone. He started the post office and had to read the letters to the townspeople. The postmaster just never stopped reading the letters throughout the years. People liked it. Bea is a direct descendant of our founder, and she's just keeping up with the tradition. I know it seems odd, but this town is close, and Bea would never read aloud something very private."

Sandra takes a deep breath and sighs. "I understand, but I don't want my mail read by anyone but me. Got it?"

Sam gives Sandra a strained grin and answers her with disappointment in his tone, "Got it. I'll speak to Bea."

Sandra calmly replies, "You had better. I would really hate to report this to the Postmaster General."

Sam, disappointed, watches Sandra walk away for a brief moment, then returns to the post office. As Sam walks in, Bea realizes by the look on his face that the conversation didn't go as well as Sam had hoped. "Well, she doesn't want anyone to read her mail, Bea."

Bea sorrowfully shakes her head. "I'm so sorry, I thought for sure Randy would have said something to her about it. I feel just awful."

Sam gives Bea a wink. "Oh, don't worry about it. Things will work out. Have faith."

Bea smiles faintly. "Thank you, Sam."

"Sure, Bea. See you later." Sam waves bye to Bea and heads out the door.

Chapter 2

Faith and Lily leave the town hall building. Faith, focusing on pulling Lily in the wagon and not on where she is going, walks right into Jake Pelsner, a handsome man in his fifties, with shoulder-length hair and an unshaven face.

"Oh, Jake, I'm so sorry. I wasn't watching where I was going."

Jake immediately looks at Lily. "That's ok. Is it Wednesday already?"

Faith replies with frustration. "No, it's still Tuesday. I put the wrong hat on her this morning, which, after today, will never happen again."

Jake laughs softly at her response. "I kind of figured that out. Listen, Faith, I was just wondering if you would like to have dinner one night?"

Faith is completely caught off guard. "Ummmm, really busy lately. Let me think about it. Okay?"

"Sure, no problem."

"Great. Have a good day, Jake."

"You too, Faith."

Faith quickly walks past Jake and immediately heads to the church where Sam works, still pulling Lily in the wagon. She walks as fast as she can, reaches the church, and walks directly into his office without knocking. Sam is reading a letter; he puts it on his desk when he sees Faith. Faith is almost out of breath as she begins to speak.

"Sam, you are never gonna believe what just happened!"

"What's going on, Faith? Are you okay?"

"No, I'm not."

"Faith, it would be nice if you would make an appointment if you need to see me. I am at work, ya know. And where is Lily?"

"She's sitting right outside the door."

Sam walks to his office door and slightly opens it to see Lily sitting in the wagon, still wearing her cowboy hat. He shakes his head and closes the door, turning back to Faith.

Faith finally catches her breath, "I know I shouldn't bother you at work, but this is an emergency."

"Okay, Faith, I'm always here for you. What is it?"

"Jake Pelsner just asked me out."

Sam realizes the situation is not a real emergency, and he smirks to himself, "So go out with him."

Faith shakes her head, "I can't."

"Why not?"

"Because I'm not ready and may never be ready to date anyone. I'm too old, and he looks like he should be playing Jesus in a miniseries. Long hair and beard, no thank you. So, when I look at him, I think of Jesus. I can't go out with Jesus."

Sam smiles again to himself. "Okay, first, he's NOT Jesus, and please never refer to him that way again. And second, it's okay not to be ready to start dating again. Just be honest with him. He's a good guy. He will understand."

Faith stares off in the distance for a second. "Well, that makes sense. Wow, this was easy. Thank you."

"You are very welcome, and please use a phone if you need advice again. I'm always here for you, Faith. And don't forget about dinner tonight at Dad's house."

"Alright. See you tonight. Oh, do I need to bring anything?"

"No. Dad is cooking a small feast. He loves to cook, and I love to eat, so we're all happy. He will have everything he needs. And Faith, please take Lily home. I'm sure she would love to get out of that wagon and out of that hat."

"Going straight home."

Faith leaves Sam's office, puts Lily in her truck, and begins the long drive home to her family farm. As she drives, she passes the church where she and David were married. Memories of her past start unexpectedly flooding back to her.

Faith remembers their wedding day, standing in front of the church as they were just pronounced man and wife. She and David were both radiant and holding hands. Faith can't help but smile.

Suddenly, Faith has a memory of her, Cricket, and David visiting her family's farm at Christmas when Cricket was about four years old. David's voice enters her mind.

"I don't understand why we have to come all this way for the holidays. Why can't we just stay home for once? You know I hate the country and all these smelly animals."

Faith remembered her response. "Look, David, you have nothing to do with your parents, and I want Cricket to know my parents—her grandparents. Besides, she loves it here. It can't always be what you want, David. Sometimes it has to be about our daughter, the one you rarely spend time with."

"Well, next holiday, you and Cricket can come alone. This is my last trip."

Tears begin to roll down Faith's face, and she wipes them away. Faith catches herself reminiscing and slightly swerves off the road. She swerves back onto the road and refocuses on getting Lily home and then making it to dinner with Sam.

Chapter 3

A few hours later, Faith arrives at Sam's father's house. She knocks on the door. "Hello. Anyone home?"

Sam opens the door. "Come on in. Dad is in the kitchen. Hello, Lily. Didn't know she was coming to dinner. I'll set an extra plate at the table." Lily walks past Sam, wearing a floppy red gardening hat. "I can see it is still Tuesday. Lily has the right hat on now."

Faith responds with a hint of disdain. "Yes, I got tired of all the hat comments. I'm sorry to bring her, but she looked too sad to leave home alone. I think she misses Mom. I'm doing my best to bond with her, but Mom has this dog very spoiled. In fact, the entire town spoils her. I can't walk two feet without someone patting her head or giving her a treat." Faith walks into the kitchen and greets Sam's father, Mr. Wright, a man in his mid-eighties. "Hello, Mr. Wright. How are you?"

"Well, if it ain't the town troublemaker." Mr. Wright laughs and hugs Faith. He looks down and sees Lily. "Good evening, councilwoman," he says, then looks back to Faith. "I'm good. How are you?"

"Oh, I'm good."

Mr. Wright, concerned, does not quite believe what Faith said. "No, really, how are you?"

"Honestly, I'm okay. Getting better every day; it's just gonna take time."

Mr. Wright turns back to preparing the meal while he speaks to Faith. "Your folks were my best friends, and I miss them every day. Listen, if you need any help with the farm, just let me know."

"Thank you, I will. The farm is actually doing quite well. Dad taught me so much when I was a kid. I take care of all the animals, and Mr. Camp farms the fields. We both make money. It's coming back to me, slowly, but I'm getting into my own routine. So, how is Kate? You're going to be a great-grandpa again, I hear."

"Yep, I am. I hope it's a boy this time. Girls are too much trouble."

Faith laughs. "That's what I hear!"

Mr. Wright laughs softly. "I remember how much trouble you and Sam got into growing up."

Sam walks in from another room and joins the conversation. "Yes, Faith. I remember you trying to convince me that a cow can be tipped over. We upset Mr. Milburn's cows, and they broke through the fence and trampled Mr. Duncan's garden. We got into so much trouble that day."

Faith jokingly snaps back, "Oh, and hot-wiring Mr. Smith's tractor was all *my* idea?"

Sam shakes his head and grins. "Who would have thought there were no brakes on that old clunker?"

Faith carries the salad bowl to the table. "Well, it would have been okay if it had just run out of gas and not run into the catfish pond."

Mr. Wright brings the last dish to the set table, claps his hands, and says, "Okay, enough memory lane talk. Let's eat."

Lily jumps up into a chair at the dining room table. Mr. Wright sets a plate with food in front of her, and she politely begins to eat each morsel. Sam looks at Lily, rolls his eyes, and then bows his head to say grace. After a hearty "Amen," they all start eating a great, home-cooked meal. They finish dinner, and Faith offers to help clean up the dishes. As Faith and Mr. Wright begin washing plates, Faith sees Sam go into the study. After all the dishes are washed and dried, Mr. Wright tells Sam and Faith good night, and he retires to bed. Faith walks into the study to see what Sam is doing. Lily follows Faith into the study, jumps up on the sofa, and immediately falls asleep. Faith can see that Sam is putting together a puzzle.

Faith walks to the table and picks up a puzzle piece. "Whatcha working on, Sam?"

"A puzzle."

Faith replies sarcastically, "You're kidding."

"I'm not kidding. Dad likes to put puzzles together, so I bought a few for him. This one, however, is mine. Here, sit down and help me."

"Sure, why not. What are we putting together?" she says as she looks for the box top to see the picture. Faith finds the box cover and realizes there is no picture on it. "Why is the box top blank?"

"Well, you don't know what you're putting together. It's a surprise. That's the fun of it."

Faith gives Sam a confused look but sits down at the table, picks up puzzle pieces, and starts to place the outer frame of the puzzle together.

Sam picks up puzzle pieces, trying to help Faith with the outer frame, and he begins to talk to Faith. "I know you've been back in Millstone for a while now, but I haven't had a chance to sit down and really have a talk with you."

"About?"

"Please, Faith, this is me you're talking to."

"Well, what do you want to know?"

Sam stops what he is doing and turns to Faith. "For starters, how are you really managing everything? You seem fine, and I know how strong you are, but I just want to make sure you're doing okay."

Faith continues to search for the puzzle pieces she needs to complete the frame. She doesn't want to give her full attention to the conversation because she knows in her heart that she isn't ready to discuss all that has happened to her, not even with Sam. "I really don't know. I was just starting to deal with David's passing; then Mom and Dad died so unexpectedly. Plus, I worry about Cricket all the time."

"You know you don't have to deal with all of this on your own. Have you been praying about it?"

Faith continues to work on the puzzle as she rolls her eyes, "Sam, I haven't prayed in years. Besides, you were always way more spiritual than me."

"That's not true. When we were kids, you invited me to church camp every year with your church. I went and loved it. You were really close to God until you moved to Chicago. What happened?"

"Life happened. David worked too much and stopped going to church with me and Cricket. I didn't want to go without him, so I just stopped going altogether. I haven't been to church in years, much less prayed. I'm doing okay by myself."

"I don't believe that, Faith. I haven't seen you show any real emotion since you came home."

Faith can feel herself becoming defensive. "I've taken on all the farm responsibilities alone. It's a lot. Cut me some slack."

"I'm not trying to put you down, Faith. But I know how much faith you had in God at one time, and I don't want you to ever lose it. It's in there somewhere, I know it. I remember the day you gave your life to Christ. Remember? We were both about twelve years old at summer church camp. The day you were saved was the happiest I had ever seen you. You were so filled with joy and the Holy Spirit. I wanted to feel what you felt so badly. Do you remember?"

Faith lowers her head and, very quietly, says, "Yes, I remember."

Sam realizes that the conversation is upsetting Faith, so he says, "Faith, will you do something for me, please?"

Faith looks directly at Sam. "Sure, if I can."

"Stop and take some time to talk to God. That's all I ask."

Faith smiles at Sam. "Okay, I will try."

"And can I ask you for another favor?"

"Of course."

"Since you live so close to Dad, can you stop by and check on him every few days?"

Faith pats Sam on the shoulder and says, "I would be honored to check in on him."

"Thank you. I'm really busy at church right now, and if you have time, work on this puzzle. It might relax you."

Faith glances at her wristwatch, "Okay. Look, I've got to head out. Early to bed, early to rise; the life of a farmer. Tell your dad again, thank you for dinner."

Sam returns to putting the puzzle pieces together and sighs. "Sure thing."

Faith drives home, thinking about all that Sam had said to her. She remembers when she gave her life to Christ and how happy she was that day. She remembers kneeling before a wooden cross with Sam before a crowd of young kids, crying tears of joy as Sam had given his life to Christ. She recalls what she said to Sam that evening. "You did it, Sam. Your name is now written in the Book of Life in Heaven. I'm so happy for you. Now you will walk with Jesus every day." She recalls the sweet smile Sam gave her while he was still kneeling before the cross, tears in his eyes.

Faith focuses on the road as a tear rolls down her face. She tries to think about something else and turns on the radio, listening to music until she arrives home. She gets Lily out of the truck, goes inside, and heads straight to bed.

Chapter 4

The next day, Faith is in town, shopping at the grocery store. As she turns down the next aisle, she sees an old friend from high school walking towards her. Dayna Dupree is not just an old friend of Faith's, but also Sam's ex-girlfriend. Dayna sees Faith and pushes her grocery basket in Faith's direction, excitedly yelling, "Faith, is that you?"

"Dayna? Wow, it's been a long time. What have you been up to?"

"Oh, we're just visiting Mom and Dad with the kids. I heard about everything that happened. You okay?"

"I'm getting there."

"We all loved your parents. I will always remember them fondly. I never met David, but, well, I've been praying for you. Are you going to church on Sunday? Ronnie and I are taking Mom and Dad and the kids."

Faith was not sure how to answer. "Maybe. I've been so busy with the farm and with driving Lily back and forth to town council meetings, I barely have time to breathe."

"I still can't believe the town voted for her to be on the council. We thought it was the funniest thing we had ever heard! I hear she's doing a really good job. Mom and Dad are always talking about it. Well, got to go. It was so good seeing you. I hope to see you at church on Sunday."

"It was good seeing you, too, Dayna."

Faith stood still for a moment. She hadn't thought about Dayna for many years. She wondered to herself why Dayna never crossed her mind, not once. Faith finishes shopping and stops in at the post office to check for any mail.

As Faith opens the doors, she greets Bea. "Morning, Bea."

"Morning, Faith. No mail today, Hun. Where is Lily?"

"I dropped her off at a doggy daycare so she can be around other dogs. She's starting to think she is human.

That's okay about the mail. I was just checking; I'm not expecting anything. Oh, guess who I ran into at the grocery store today?" Before Bea could answer, Faith says, "Dayna Dupree."

"I heard she was in town visiting her parents."

"I was surprised to see her. She looks great. Funny how I forgot about her. We were all fairly close in high school when she and Sam were dating. They were together for five years. I always thought they would get married."

"We all thought the same thing."

Faith starts to remember more about Dayna. "She was so heartbroken when Sam went off to Bible College. Then, when he graduated and became a missionary, it was just too much for her. I know Sam tried to keep the relationship going, but she wanted nothing to do with being a missionary's girlfriend and possibly a missionary's wife one day. She expected Sam to return from college and settle back down here in Millstone."

"I know. But she married an attorney and has three kids. She seems happy. That kind of life suits her. Her mother is always telling me about the exciting dinner parties that they have for the elite; you know, congress-men and oil tycoons, those rich high society types. I'm happy for her."

Faith thinks for a moment before replying. "You're right. That type of life suits her. She wouldn't have been happy traveling with Sam in the vastly remote places he was sent to all over the world."

"Few women could have managed that, Hun."

"I know I couldn't have done it!" Faith says as she looks at the Fall Festival poster on the wall.

Bea sees Faith reading the poster. "So, are you excited about the Fall Festival next month?"

"Are we still doing that thing? Wow, that brings back a lot of memories. Who's in charge this year?"

"Sam has been in charge for a few years now. If you want to help, just get with Sam, and he will tell you what to do. I'm in charge of getting all the food organized. Mr. Trotter sets up the games and other activities. I believe we still need help with the decorations, but I'm not sure. Like I said, get with Sam. Maybe Lily can make a speech. She is the favorite member of the town council."

Faith looks at Bea with absolutely no expression. "You get funnier every time I see you."

"I hope so. A sense of humor is the only way to get through the day, sometimes."

Faith looks at the large clock on the wall. "It's nearing lunchtime, Bea. Would you like to meet me for lunch and grab a bite to eat?"

"Sure. I've been hankering for a chicken-fried steak at Nolan's Restaurant all morning. Best chicken-fried steak in town. My mouth is watering just thinking about it."

"Great, my treat. I just have to pick up Lily at doggy daycare. How about we meet in an hour?"

"Sounds good, Hun."

Faith gets in her truck and drives through town toward the doggy daycare. She sees Sam on the top of the church. She stops the truck and yells to Sam, "What are you doing up there?"

Sam stops working when he hears Faith and yells back, "Fixing the roof!"

Faith continues to project her voice so Sam can hear her. "Aren't there professionals that can do that for you?"

Sam nods his head yes and yells back, "Yes, but I know how to do it, and besides, it will save the church money."

"I really don't like this. Please be careful, Sam. Hey, if you need help with this Fall Festival, let me know."

Sam waves his hammer and says, "I will. Okay. See ya."

Faith continues to drive to the doggy daycare center when she sees Jake leaving the hardware store. She looks ahead and speeds up, hoping he won't see her. Faith arrives at the doggy day care and enters the building. Standing at the counter is a young girl about eighteen years old with purple hair.

"I'm here to pick up Lilly," Faith says to the girl at the counter. "How did she do today? Did she make any friends?"

The young girl answers Faith in a completely emotionless and monotone manner. "Not really. She had absolutely no desire to socialize with the other dogs. We tried to engage her, but she refused. And the other dogs didn't seem interested in her either. It might be the hat."

Faith starts to chuckle, but the girl keeps a straight face, not showing any emotion at all. She realizes the girl isn't joking and quickly says, "Oh, you're serious?"

"Yes." Another staff member escorts Lily to the front counter. Lily is wearing a baseball cap and a handkerchief around her neck. She sees Faith, gets overly excited, and wags her tail, knocking over a dog shampoo display. Faith picks it up and fixes the display.

Faith looks down at Lily, "Come on, Lily; let's go get some lunch."

Faith walks Lily to the truck, lifts Lily, and puts her in the passenger seat. Then, Faith gets in the truck and looks at Lily. "So, you didn't enjoy getting to know the other dogs? It's okay. Maybe we can try again next week. And for the record, I like your hat." Lily looks back at Faith and wags her tail. "We are meeting Bea for lunch, so behave, please."

Faith drives to the restaurant and parks, then she and Lily go inside. She sees Bea sitting at a table, and they walk to join her. "I'm glad I made it on time."

Bea smiles. "Oh, I just got here myself."

The restaurant owner, Nolan, comes over to the table. He begins to speak to Lily.

"Well, it's not every day we get celebrities in here,

especially a well-known and loved council member. What can I get you to drink?"

Faith looks at the menu, then back at Nolan and says, "I'll have a glass of sweet tea."

Bea joins in. "Me, too."

Nolan looks at Faith and says, "I was actually talking to Councilwoman Lily."

The customers start to laugh, and Bea begins to chuckle before saying, "You're kidding, right?"

Faith, in disbelief, puts down the menu and addresses Nolan, "I've known you since kindergarten, and you're waiting on the dog first?"

Nolan replies with a straight face. "Sorry, our town council members get priority service."

The restaurant customers all begin to laugh again.

Nolan looks at his notepad and reads aloud what he has written. "One water for Councilwoman Lily and two sweet teas for her guests. I'll be back to take your orders. And by the way, all town officials eat for free, so no charge for you, Miss Lily. You can order anything on the menu." He purposely ignores Bea and Faith, and once again, the customers laugh. Faith realizes that Nolan is just having fun and joking at her expense. Faith turns around, looks at all the customers, and says sarcastically, "Ha, ha, everyone in this town is so funny." The customers laugh again.

Bea grabs her napkin and quietly says, "Well, he had me going there for a minute."

Faith, wanting to change the subject, says to Bea, "As I was driving over here, guess who I saw on the roof of the church?"

"No need to guess, it's Sam, I saw him up there yesterday."

"Kind of dangerous, isn't it?"

"Yes, but you know Sam; once he makes up his mind to do something, there is no talking him out of it."

Nolan comes back with two teas and a small bowl of water. He places the drinks on the table. Faith and Bea both thank him, and he takes their food orders. Both Bea and Faith order chicken-fried steaks, and Faith orders Lily the child's chicken nugget plate.

Faith wants to continue the conversation about Sam and the roof. She says, "Okay, back to Sam, I'm really afraid for his safety being on that steep roof."

Bea just shakes her head. "Good luck talking him out of it."

Nolan brings out the food, places Lily's plate first on the table, and pats her head. Lily delicately eats one nugget at a time, seemingly enjoying every bite until Nolan slips a sugar cookie onto her plate. Lily eats it in one swift gulp. Faith and Bea shake their heads and begin eating their meal while chatting about other things happening in Millstone. Before long, lunchtime was about over, and Bea had to get back to the post office. They say their goodbyes and head in different directions.

Chapter 5

The next morning, Faith is out working on the farm. She sees Jake drive up. He gets out of his truck and walks over to Faith, who is cleaning out goat pens.

Faith puts down her rake and greets Jake. "Hi. What brings you out this way?"

"Well, I thought I would stop by and see if you made up your mind about having dinner with me."

Faith replies as politely as she can, "I don't think so, Jake."

"Is it because I look like Jesus?"

Faith is completely caught off guard by Jake's comment. All she can say is "Umm ..."

Jake chortles, realizing that she is speechless after what he said. "It's okay. I heard that might be the reason."

"Guess you spoke to Sam about this. Traitor," she says under her breath.

"Well, he is my pastor, Faith."

Faith decided to just come out with it and be honest. "Look, Jake, I'm just not ready to see anyone. I may never be ready. Dating at my age is the farthest thing from my mind right now. I'm trying to keep the farm afloat, and I'm still in the grieving process for my parents and David. I hope you understand."

Jake gave Faith a soft smile. "I do. Well, if you change your mind, you know where I am."

Faith, feeling relieved, says, "Yes, I do. Thanks for stopping by and for being so understanding."

Jake nods his head, gets in his truck, and drives away. Faith continues to work on the farm, performing every task, whether it be vital or menial. She walks into the goat pen, and Lily follows her in, barking and chasing the goats. The goats start running in Faith's direction and push her down in the mud. Lily, realizing that Faith has fallen, immediately stops what she is doing, walks up to Faith, and sits down directly in front of her as if she is waiting for Faith to get up. Lily is wearing a pink bonnet with polka dots, now covered in mud. Faith looks at Lily with a disgusted look on her face. She gets up and realizes she is also covered in mud from head to toe. She walks to the house, with Lily following her. Faith cleans up Lily as best she can, strips down to her undergarments, leaves her muddy clothes on the back porch, and heads to her bathroom to shower.

After her shower, she gets dressed and heads to the kitchen to make something to eat. As she walks through the den, something familiar catches her eye. There, on the table between two recliners, is one of her mother's many Bibles. Faith picks it up and slowly flips through the pages. Lily, looking out the window, starts barking at a squirrel in the front yard, distracting Faith. She walks to the window to see what Lily is barking at and realizes it's nothing of importance, so she continues to the kitchen to cook a simple meal. After lunch, she heads back outside to finish her daily chores, completing them just before dusk. Faith is too tired to do anything but sleep, so she and Lily retire to bed.

The next morning, Faith wakes up with a fever. She calls Sam on the phone.

Sam, looking at the number on his phone, answers, "Good morning, Faith."

"I'm sick."

"What do you mean by sick?"

"I mean, I'm sick, sick; fever, body aches, probably the flu or a bug. Can you please pick up Lily and drive her to the town hall for the weekly council meeting?"

Sam, not wanting to drive Lily to the meeting, replies,

"I think the council can do without her for one meeting. And I heard most of the staff at the doggy daycare center were sent home with the flu. That's probably where you picked up the bug."

"Oh, that's just great to know. Look, Sam, I know you think this whole 'dog as a council member' is ridiculous, but the town loves Lily. Please?"

Sam lets out a huge sigh. "I'm on my way."

"Thank you, Sam. I owe you one."

"See you in a bit. Make sure Lily is ready and wearing the correct hat for today."

Sam arrives at Faith's farm, where she is on the porch wearing her pajamas wrapped up in a blanket. Lily waits patiently for Sam, wearing a straw hat with spring flowers around the brim. Sam sees Lily as he drives up.

"It must be Thursday," Sam says, knowing Lily wears that hat only on Thursdays. "Come on, Lily. Let's get this show on the road." Sam opens the passenger door, and Lily runs to the truck, jumps in, and begins wagging her tail. Sam grabs the seatbelt, and Lily sits so he can put it around her to ensure that she remains safe on their drive to town. Faith and Sam wave to each other, and Faith returns inside to rest in bed.

Faith immediately falls asleep and begins to dream. She dreams of Sam and her as children, running through the woods at church camp. She feels peaceful and happy. She sees the younger versions of themselves, swimming, boating, playing sports, and praying. Then, out of the blue, Faith sees her parents swerving to miss a head-on collision and driving off the road. The car flips numerous times.

Faith wakes up frantically. She realizes she was dreaming and tries to calm herself. Faith didn't actually see her parents' car wreck, but she dreams about how it might have occurred, and it haunts her that she wasn't there for them.

Faith walks to her bathroom to wash her face from all the sweating of a bad dream. Then she hears a familiar vehicle drive up and park in her driveway. She grabs a blanket, wraps it around her, and walks to the front door. Just as she suspected, it's Jake. Jake yells from the front screen door, "Hey, it's Jake. Sam said you were sick, so I brought you some soup. May I come in?"

Faith reaches the door and says, "Sure, but I think I have the flu, and I don't want you to catch it."

"Oh, don't worry about me. I had it a few weeks ago. I'll be fine."

"This is really thoughtful of you, Jake. Come on in and have a seat."

Faith opens the door, and Jake walks in and sits down on the sofa. Faith, pale and weak and still wrapped in a blanket, sits in one of two big leather recliners. Jake hands Faith the chicken soup and a spoon. Faith takes the soup and spoon and places them on the table between the two recliners. There is an uneasy silence between them, so Faith starts small talk.

"So, what brought you to Millstone, Jake?"

"I guess Sam didn't tell you?"

"No, Sam hasn't told me much about you."

"Well, I met Sam in college. I was studying to be a minister, too. Sam and I went on missionary trips together. He talked about his hometown all the time. After 25 years of missionary work, I decided to retire early. I didn't want to go back to New York, so I came here and fell in love with small-town country life. I bought a farm and learned the ropes, and here I am."

"Wow. That's really amazing, Jake."

"My dad was a missionary for many years, then became a full-time pastor of a church in Kansas, so it just made sense for me to follow in his footsteps. That and knowing it was God's plan for me also."

"How did you know that it was God's plan and not your plan?"

"Well, when you walk closely with Christ, you learn how he speaks to you. He opened many doors for me, and I willingly walked through them, not knowing what was on the other side. I trusted Him. God knew I had a passion for helping people, and I loved traveling to the most remote places on Earth, teaching people about Jesus Christ. He made it all happen. I spent a lot of time planting food and working on the land. I also learned about farming from the other missionaries. God knew my heart and knew what would make me happy, so He put His plan in motion, and I followed Him. When He led me to retire early, I came here to become an organic farmer. I still spend a couple of weeks each year traveling with Sam to help support other missionaries, then I come back to teach kids about Jesus as the youth minister at our church here in Millstone."

"Wow, you've led an amazing life, Jake. But neither you nor Sam ever got married. How come? Sorry, is that too personal of a question?"

"No, it's okay, I don't mind. I guess Sam never married because he gives all his time and energy to God. As a missionary, not many women want to travel through jungles and other places in the world trying to help bring people to Christ. Maybe God will send someone to him now that he's settled as a church pastor. As for me, I was married. But my wife passed away many years ago while giving birth. I lost them both."

"Oh, no. I am so sorry, Jake. If I had known any of this, I wouldn't have ever mentioned it to you. I'm so sorry; I feel terrible."

"I appreciate that, but it was a long time ago. Don't give it a second thought. Well, I need to get going. Is there anything else I can do for you?"

"No, I'll be fine in a few days. Thank you for stopping by and for the soup, Jake."

"Sure. If you need anything, please let me know. I'll be glad to help out in any way."

"Thank you again, Jake."

Jake leaves the house and walks to his truck as Sam is driving up to the house with Lily. They wave at each other before Jake drives away.

Lily and Sam enter the house. Lily jumps up on the sofa where Faith is now sitting, wrapped in a blanket and blowing her nose. Sam keeps his distance to not catch whatever Faith has contracted. Faith grabs another tissue, blows her nose, and looks up at Sam. "Well, I just had an interesting conversation with Jake earlier."

"Really? Good."

"Why didn't you tell me about your history with Jake and about him losing his family?"

"Because it wasn't my story to tell, Faith."

"Do you always have to be so honorable?"

Sam smirks and changes the subject. "Feeling any better?"

"Not really. I'm sure if I just rest, I will kick this thing in a few days."

"Okay. If you need anything, just call me or Dad. Okay?"

"Will do, buckaroo."

Sam gives a playful grin as he leaves, remembering that Faith called him either buckaroo or dude ranch when they were kids.

The next morning, Faith feels slightly better than she did the day before. Regardless of how she feels, she knows there are animals to feed, milk, and turn out to pasture. She gets dressed in overalls and a cap, heads to the barn, and starts filling feed buckets to begin her morning routine. Faith could have called Sam, Jake, or even Mr. Wright to help with her farm chores, but it never crossed her mind. Faith loves the farm and feels blessed to be back home. She loves the hard work and being surrounded by all the animals, which makes her feel that she belongs there more than anywhere else. Her happiest memories are all around her, in the pastures where the animals graze, to the overgrown grass in the arena where she ran barrels in her youth.

Faith walks up to Bella's stall and places a halter on her so that she can walk her to the pasture to graze. Bella was Cricket's pony, a little, stocky, black and white mare, nearly thirty-five years old. Bella was a birthday gift from Faith's parents to Cricket the summer Cricket turned five. That was the year Faith and Cricket stayed at the farm all summer, as David was working all the time and rarely had time for them. Faith had awakened one morning and, out of the blue, decided to spend the entire summer on the farm with her parents. She worked from home for a large investment company, so she knew she could continue to work remotely on her parents' farm. She had packed enough clothes for herself and Cricket and left a note for David, as he wouldn't answer his phone when Faith tried to call him. She had no choice but to leave sticky notes all over the bathroom mirror, indicating where they had gone and when they would return. It was two days before David noticed the notes and realized Faith and Cricket were not in their home in Chicago. Two whole days! He was furious that they had gone to Texas for the summer, but Faith was unfazed by his anger. She just wanted to be with Cricket on the farm, teaching her to ride her pony and spend quality time with her parents.

As she takes the halter off Bella, she remembers her own first pony when she was a child and how much she loved him. When she was little, she couldn't wait to wake up, eat breakfast, finish her chores, then head out to the barn so she could spend all day with Champ, her fat, little dapple grey pony. She would ride him in the pastures and down to Sam's house, where they would all rest under a tree, talking about God and how excited they were about going to church camp in the weeks to come. Eventually, as Faith grew older, her dad bought her a Quarter Horse, but they kept Champ until he passed away on the farm from old age. It was the first time Faith felt the pain of losing something that she dearly loved, and it took her a long time to get over losing him. She would pray to God to take care of Champ in Heaven until she could be there to take care of him herself.

Faith became very close to Cisco, her Quarter Horse. She and Cisco participated in the Texas Youth Rodeo throughout junior high and high school. She loved him with all her heart, and when she went off to college, her heart broke into a million pieces, for leaving him was one of the hardest things she ever had to do. She remembers the day he passed away on the farm. Faith and Cricket were at the farm for the Easter holiday, and once again, David stayed in Chicago.

Faith went out that morning to feed Cisco and brush him. When she finished, she put a halter on him and walked him to the pasture to graze. As they walked side by side, Cisco continued to nuzzle Faith's shoulder, trying to keep her attention. When she closed the pasture gate, she removed his halter and rubbed his head. She told him what a wonderful horse he was and how much she loved him. Faith trusted Cisco with every ounce of her being, and before Cricket was old enough to walk, she sat on Cisco's back as Faith walked him around in a circle. Cricket was unafraid and loved every minute of riding on the big bay horse.

As Faith began to walk towards the pasture gate, Cisco followed her, still trying to keep her attention. Faith decided to spend the morning with Cisco, walking through the pasture, talking to him about her life and all she was going through with David. Faith needed to tell someone about it. Sam and Faith were still close, but

Sam was in Africa as a missionary, and it wasn't like Faith could just pick up the phone and call him. So she talked to Cisco that day, her kind and trusted friend. Eventually, Cricket joined them, and they both rubbed his head and patted his neck. Cisco began grazing and focused on eating the thick, green pasture hay that surrounded him, so Faith and Cricket went back to the farmhouse.

Hours later, something told Faith to check on Cisco, so she watched Cisco graze through the kitchen window, then saw him lie down. She knew, for some reason, that he would never get up again and would be gone forever. It was the second time in her life to lose something that she loved dearly, and even though he was very old, she didn't see it coming; she didn't expect to ever lose him. And when she did, it broke her heart.

Faith called David to inform him of Cisco's passing and how much she was hurting. When David answered his phone, he could tell she had been crying. When she told him that Cisco had died, he said, "It's just a horse. You really are overreacting about it. Time to grow up, Faith, and care about more important things." At that moment, the feelings she had for David changed. It wasn't something she could help; it just happened. As bad as things were with David at that point, they would get worse, and their relationship would never recover. But Faith was strong, and she stayed with David for Cricket's sake, keeping her problems and her pain to herself.

Faith caught herself reminiscing about the past, failing to understand why her mind kept taking her to those dark, painful memories. She decided to focus solely on finishing her chores without remembering anything that might bring her pain. As Faith completed her work, she could feel herself growing weak and feverish, so she decided to return to the house and go to bed.

Chapter 6

week later, Faith is completely over the flu and pulling Lily in the wagon through town. Lily is wearing a pink beret and a string of fake pearls around her neck. Faith enters the post office to check for any mail.

Bea greets them jovially. "Good morning, ladies. You look quite sophisticated with that beret, Lily. It must be Friday."

"Morning, Bea, and yes, it is 'Beret Friday,'" Faith says sarcastically. "Any mail, Bea?"

"Yep. Your brother isn't coming after all, hun. He eloped and is now on his honeymoon in Alaska."

"You've got to be kidding me."

"I wish I were dear. Here's his letter," Bea says as she hands Faith the letter from her brother. As Faith reads the letter, Sandra Simmons walks in to pick up her mail.

Bea gives Sandra a friendly greeting. "Good morning, Mrs. Simmons. I'll get your mail right away. Here you go."

"Thank you," Sandra says as she takes her mail and leaves.

Faith looks up from reading the letter and watches Sandra walk out the door. "I heard she doesn't like our town tradition. It never bothered Randy."

"Well, small town life isn't for everyone," says Bea.

"Apparently not. Well, we are off to the elementary school. Councilwoman Lily is judging the art contest."

"Oh my, that's wonderful," Bea says as she walks over to pat Lily on the head.

"Yep. They requested her specifically. Not sure how I'm going to pull this one off."

"Maybe she will place her paw on the best one or point with her tail."

Faith shrugs her shoulders and says, "Maybe. Who knows?

This dog's public service career is really starting to consume too much of my time. I'll let you know how it goes."

Bea chuckles. "Please do."

Faith leaves the post office, pulling Lily in the wagon.

They hurry to the elementary school so that Lily can judge the art contest. Lily chooses the winner by placing her paw on the painting. After the winner is announced, Faith leaves the school and places Lily in the truck. Faith shakes her head in amazement because Lily did, in fact, choose the best painting.

Faith begins her drive back to the farm. Suddenly, she hears a large pop; her tire has blown. Faith gets out of the truck and simply stares at the blown tire, shaking her head.

She hears a familiar voice from behind her. "I'm really not stalking you, Faith. Need any help?"

"Oh, it's okay, Jake, I can change a tire. I'm just staring at it, hoping this isn't a precursor for how the rest of my day will go."

"I have no doubt that you can change a tire, but please allow me to help."

"Thank you, Jake. I really do appreciate your help," Faith says as she watches Jake get the spare tire and jack from the bed of her farm truck.

"No problem. I'm always happy to help."

Faith was actually glad that Jake showed up to help. It gave her a chance to keep an eye on Lily, who was intently watching a cat perched in a nearby tree from the passenger side of the truck. It also gave her a moment to talk to Jake. Knowing the pain he suffered gave Faith a different perspective on him. She started to look past the long hair and unshaven face to see a kind and gentle soul who is always thoughtful and helpful. She could see why Jake and Sam were good friends. Both men were honorable, and both had a moral compass that always pointed to 'Do the right thing.' Faith still had issues because of David, but deep down inside, she knew that there were good guys out there. She just wasn't ready to go down that road again, not now, maybe never.

Faith felt the uneasiness of silence, so she started small talk.

"So, how is your farm doing, Jake?

"Really well. I've been lucky to get advice from Sam's dad when I needed it."

"Yep. Mr. Wright is really a great farmer and a really good man. Mr. Wright had always been there for me and my parents. They were all the best of friends. I know he misses them dearly. When Sam's mom passed away, my parents were there for Mr. Wright and Sam. It was really a tough time for everyone. My parents and Sam's parents grew up together, so you can imagine the bond they shared."

"I can imagine that and how hard that must have been for you all. There, all done," Jake says as he eases down the jack.

"Wow, that was really fast. I can't thank you enough, Jake. You're really a good guy."

"I try to be. Okay, have a good rest of your day."

"Thank you. I will. You have a good day too, Jake."

As Faith watched Jake drive away, she thought about his significant loss. She couldn't imagine ever getting over losing a spouse and a child at the same time. It was an awful thought. She wondered how Jake could remain a kind and gentle person rather than a man scorned and full of disdain because of losing all that really mattered to him. She shook her head and walked back to the driver's side of her truck. There was Lily, patiently hanging out the passenger door window, wagging her tail, and waiting to go home.

The drive back to the farm was quiet. Faith continued to ponder why Jake seemed happy and whole, and she felt somber and half-hearted. They arrive at the farm, and Faith walks into the house and straight to the kitchen to make something to eat. Once again, she notices her mother's Bible, but she turns and focuses on her meal.

Faith decides to start going through her parents' things, since her brother isn't coming to help her. She opens boxes and envelopes, making sure she hasn't missed anything. She sees a photo album, begins turning the pages, and realizes it's photos of her parents' wedding day. Faith hadn't seen that album in many, many years. Page by page, the album returns her to a time when she didn't know her parents, when her parents were young, carefree, and just starting their lives together. Faith lights up with delight as she sees a photo of her mother, Katie, in her wedding dress, featuring white lace from the top of the veil to the bottom of the hem, extending to the end of the long, flowing train. Her mother was absolutely beautiful. Being of Irish descent, her mother's fiery red hair and emerald green eyes were so stunning that one could hardly stop staring at her, either in a photo or in person. Faith's mother was a wonderful person full of love, positivity, and creativity. She was a woman of great strength and faith who saw the best in everyone, and if you needed her, she would be there. She was an amazing mother and wife, always putting Christ first in her life.

Faith turns her attention to the tall, thin man standing next to her mother in the photo: Walter, her sweet, lovable father. Faith had never seen her father in a suit other than in this picture and, of course, on Faith's own wedding day as he walked her down the aisle to give her away to David. His closet was full of overalls and work shirts, and he was rarely seen wearing anything else. He dressed for the job he loved and could never see himself doing anything other than farming. He loved the Lord, loved the land, and loved his family more than life itself. He never complained about working hard; instead, he thanked God that he had work at hand. He never complained about what her mother cooked; rather, he felt blessed that there was food on the table to eat. Both Faith's parents were raised in poverty and never forgot where they came from or how hard they had to work to make a comfortable life for Faith and Ben.

She sees photos of her and her brother when they were little. There were numerous photos of holidays and family vacations. She couldn't help but smile as she looked at the photos of her life before she moved away to Chicago. Then, she noticed another album. It was filled with pictures of her and David on their wedding day. She closed the album quickly so as to not be reminded of that part of her life. Then she found a small photo album. Inside were photos of her and Sam, of their school days and church camp. She sees a photo of her and Sam kneeling before a cross at church camp. She realizes that was the day she gave her life to Christ. Tears fill her eyes as she begins to remember how happy she was and how close she was to God.

Suddenly, the house phone rings and Faith answers, "Hello?"

"Hey, just wondering if you were serious about helping with the Fall Festival."

Faith, recognizing Sam's voice, replies, "Of course. When is it again?"

"The end of next month. I just want to give everyone time to get things in order. Do you think you could get some animals rounded up for a petting zoo for the kids?"

"Yes, oh, thank goodness, something easy for me to do. I was afraid you wanted me to bake or something. I have several baby goats, baby chicks, and two baby ducks. I'm sure I can borrow a bunny from Bea since she raises them. And of course, Lily will be available for autographs."

"I'm sure she would love that! Sounds good. Thank you."

"So glad to be able to help, Sam."

"I'll give you more details in a week or so. I really want this year to be special. Your parents always helped so much, and I want to honor them by doing the best festival ever."

"Sounds really good, Sam. It will be great. Talk to you later."

"Okay, bye, Faith."

Chapter 7

The next morning, Faith and Lily drive into town. Faith parks her truck directly in front of the town hall building. She gets out, puts Lily in her wagon, and walks a few blocks to the post office. As they arrive, Bea is waiting at the door and helps Faith pull the wagon with Lily in it through the door. Faith greets Bea warmly.

"Morning, Bea. Thank you for helping with the door."

"Morning, Faith. It's no trouble at all. Good morning, Councilwoman Lily," Bea says as she laughs.

"Gee, Bea, that never gets old for you, does it?"

"Nope. Never does and never will." Bea chuckles again as Faith shakes her head.

"Well, I was hoping to get some news from my long-lost brother. I need help going through our parents' things and making the house more like mine than theirs. Not to be disrespectful, but Mom's taste in furnishings was quite different from mine. If I'm going to make Millstone my home for good, then I need to get my things from Chicago. Please tell me I have a letter from him because he won't answer the phone."

"You do, Hun. He sent you a postcard from Rome."

"Rome, seriously? I thought he was in Alaska."

Bea hands Faith the postcard. "Yes, he was, but it seems like they are on an extended honeymoon."

"Good grief. Rome? I'm gonna need to have a lengthy conversation with him very soon. I guess I know now why he isn't returning my phone calls."

"Hmm. Ben must be terribly busy eating spaghetti," Bea says, laughing.

"Ha, ha, very funny. I'm sure that's exactly what they are spending all their time doing: eating pasta. Okay, Bea, see you later. Got to get Lily to another meeting."

"Make us proud, Lily," Bea says, chuckling to herself again.

As Faith walks to the town hall building, she passes by the church. She sees Sam on the roof again and stops to talk to him. Faith raises her voice so Sam can hear her. "Seriously, Sam? Please get a professional to do this roofing project. It makes me extremely nervous."

Sam yells so Faith can hear him as well. "I'm fine. I know what I'm doing. I want it completed before the festival next month. Have some faith, Faith."

"Ha, ha, very funny. Like I've never heard that one before. Okay. I'll see you later. PLEASE BE CARE-FUL!"

After the council meeting, Faith gets in her truck and drives home to the farm. As she walks through the front door, the house phone rings again.

Faith, once again not knowing who it might be, answers, "Hello?"

"I was just wondering if you and Lily want to join me and Dad for dinner this evening?"

"Sure, Sam. Hey, why have you been calling the house phone and not my cell?"

"I keep leaving my cell phone on the church roof."

"Well, it's a good thing my parents' phone number never changed. They had the same number since they took over the farm from my grandpa when they first got married. Wow, that's crazy how some things never change and how some things always change."

"Well, I know one thing that never changes."

"What's that, Sam?"

"God. He never changes. He is the same today as He was when He created this amazing world we live in six thousand years ago. Have you thought about what we talked about?"

"You mean, have I started praying? Not yet. Hey, if I don't get some things done around here, I'll be late for dinner. I got to go. See you soon."

"Sure thing. See you in a bit."

Faith and Lily arrive for dinner at Mr. Wright's home. Sam opens the door to let them inside. He is amused when he sees Lily wearing a straw hat adorned with daisies and yellow and white ribbons.

"Hey, after dinner, do you want to help me with this puzzle I've been working on?"

"Sure, Sam, why not?"

Faith and Sam finish dinner, and they go into the study to work on the puzzle. They begin putting puzzle pieces in place. They work in silence until Faith starts to ask Sam questions that she had wanted to ask him for years.

"Sam, why did you become a minister? We never really talked about it. You could have done anything with your life."

"I know, and I did exactly what I wanted to do with my life by becoming a minister. Haven't you ever felt like there is something out there bigger and more important than yourself?"

"No, not really. I mean, I haven't really thought about it."

"Well, I did and still do. I wanted to help people and bring them closer to God. To me, it's the most important thing in the world. We are only here on this Earth for a brief time, and we need to bring as many people to Christ as we possibly can."

"I guess. I always knew you were religious. I just didn't think that you were going to dedicate your life to your religion."

"Faith, it's not about being religious; it's about having a personal relationship with God and walking with Him daily. It's about giving your life to Him and trusting Him in each and every part of your life. God has a plan for each of us, and we need to trust His plan, even when we don't understand it."

"How are we supposed to do that?"

Sam picks up the puzzle pieces and says, "Look, when you start to put a puzzle together, what are the pieces you use first?"

"The edges are first. You put all the edges together and you form a frame."

"Right! Imagine that the outer edges of the puzzle, or the frame, are your Christian faith."

Faith, sounding unsure of herself, answers, "Okay."

Sam picks up a puzzle piece and puts it in place. "When you allow God to use His plan for you in your life, He places all the pieces in the puzzle one by one. When we don't allow God to work His plan for us, the pieces sit on the outside of the puzzle, never to be used. But when we trust Him and allow Him to work His plan, the pieces are placed inside the frame, and each piece starts to form a picture. It's the picture of God's plan for our life."

"Well, what if God's plan isn't something that I want to happen in my life?"

"That's the best part of God's plan. He knows us so well that He knows what will make us happy. He knows us better than we know ourselves. His plan for us is perfect and always right. God will open doors for you. You just need to have the faith and the courage to walk through them."

"How will I know when He opens a door for me?"

"Well, when you read His word and walk by faith, you will get closer to Him. Things will begin to happen in your life; doors will open, opportunities will appear from nowhere. You will know what He wants you to do. The first step is to trust Him. You need to talk to Him."

"Sam, it's been a long time since I've prayed. I just don't have that kind of faith anymore."

"You will. I've been praying for you for many years."

"For many years?"

"Yes, I've never stopped praying for you, Faith."

"For what it's worth, thank you. Just don't expect a miracle with me. By the way, what is the picture of this puzzle we are putting together?"

"I already told you; I don't know. It's a surprise. That's the fun of it."

"Okay, okay, but it would be a lot easier if we knew what the picture looked like."

"Patience."

"The story of my life, patience."

Faith is quiet for a moment as she puts the puzzle pieces in place. Then, with a soft yet serious look, she begins to ask Sam more questions.

"Sam, why didn't you ever marry? It's hard to believe that you never found someone to love in all your travels."

"Well, it wasn't God's plan for me."

"Uggg! What does that mean anyway!"

Sam manages a short laugh before he replies. "Look, if God had wanted me to get married and have a family, then He would have sent a woman to me who wanted to be a missionary like me. I love my work; it is truly rewarding. And I have dated here and there, but not one woman understood my job, nor did they want that kind of life. Not everyone is meant to get married and have a family."

"Do you miss not having a family?"

"You can't miss what you've never had, Faith. And nor do I regret not pursuing that life. Believe it or not, I have a family; my dad, you, my friends, and my church members are my family. Just because I'm not romantically involved with someone right now doesn't mean I'm lonely either. I have a remarkably busy and full life that makes me happy. God knows my heart, and He knows what makes me happy. His plan is always the right plan."

"So, you're saying that you are just as happy or happier now than you would have been having a family? And God created this life plan because He knew that being a missionary was truly where your heart was at the time?"

"Absolutely. And now my heart is being a pastor here in my hometown. If my heart ever changes to desire having a family, then I know that is the next step in God's plan for me. Honestly, now that I'm not traveling as a missionary, the thought of meeting someone has crossed my mind."

"Really? Well, the new teller at the bank keeps asking me about you."

"The brunette with green eyes?"

"That would be the one. You should ask her out."

"I'll take your advice under advisement, and I'll pray about it."

"Wow, you really do trust God, don't you?"

"My trust in God is absolute. It never wavers. Faith, I want you to put more trust in God. Remember, His plan is like a puzzle. The more you allow Him to work His plan in your life, the more puzzle pieces are used. Soon, you will begin to see the picture of your life. It will be a life that truly makes you happy. And remember, it is never too late to allow God to implement the plan

He set for you."

"I'll try, Sam. I promise."

"Well, it starts with prayer and reading His word."

"I know."

"Oh, and think about attending church. I hear the pastor is amazing."

"Ha, ha. If he doesn't say so himself."

Sam grins playfully. "Oh, he says it all the time."

"Okay, I'll be there on Sunday."

"Great. And after the service, we are having a meeting about the Fall Festival. I really want it to be outstanding this year."

"Sounds good. Well, I'm off. See you tomorrow."

"Good night, Faith."

Chapter 8

$\mathcal{F}$aith and Lily arrived home, and Faith couldn't stop thinking about everything Sam said about prayer and God's plan. She decided to box up a few more of her parents' things. She found things that she could never part with and others that she couldn't wait to put up for sale. She also thought about how to retrieve her belongings from the storage unit in Chicago. And of course, she calls Sam for advice.

Sam is still awake. "Hello?"

"Hey, it's me."

"You're still awake, Faith?"

"Yes, sorry, did I wake you?"

"No, I'm still awake as well."

"I have a situation. I need to fly to Chicago and get my things out of the storage unit and move them down here."

"Okay, hire a moving company."

"I plan on doing that, but I was wondering if you would fly up with me? I really don't want to do this alone."

"I would love to, but I can't right now. I'm still finishing up the roof work on the church and making plans for the Fall Festival. Now isn't a good time. Can we go in a couple of months?"

"I really want to get closure on Chicago and focus on my life here. Plus, I'm tired of paying an outrageous sum of money every month for this storage unit. I can go alone, but it's just the memories I want to avoid."

"Whether you go alone or not, the memories will be there."

"I know. I keep putting it off, and I need to just get it done. What you said about God's plan for me really made sense. I need to move forward. I thought about leaving in a few days."

"Are you trying to avoid coming to church on Sunday, Faith?"

"Of course not. I was boxing up some of my parents' things and realized I still have all my things in Chicago. I really need to get closure on my life in Chicago and focus on my life here."

"Well, I completely agree with you, but I just can't leave that soon. If you really feel you need to do this now, maybe Jake can accompany you."

"Really, Jake? Seriously, Sam, have you lost your mind? I'm not taking Jake."

"Get over whatever issue you have with Jake and take him to Chicago. He will be a tremendous help to you, and I trust him to look out for you. He's a good guy. If it's too awkward to ask him yourself, I'll be happy to ask him as a favor to me."

"Okay, Sam, please call him. Thank you, and for the record, I don't have an issue with Jake. He really is a good guy. Thank you. Good night."

"Glad to hear it. Good night, Faith."

The next morning, Faith is outdoors performing farm chores when she hears her cell phone ring. She reaches into her overalls for her phone and sees a number she doesn't recognize, but answers the call. "Hello?"

"Good morning, Faith; it's Jake. Sam gave me your number; hope you don't mind. He said you needed some assistance in Chicago."

"Um, yes. Look, Jake, I know it's a real imposition, so if you can't go, it's totally fine."

"No, no, I'd love to go. I need a short vacation, and I've never been to Chicago. When do we leave?"

"Honestly, as soon as possible. I just need to get my things out of storage and hire a moving company to drive them all down here."

"Great! I'm ready when you are."

"Thank you, Jake. I really appreciate it."

"Not a problem. Happy to do it."

Faith makes all the necessary arrangements for their trip to Chicago. She is actually glad that she doesn't have to go alone. The next morning, they meet at the airport and board the plane. Faith and Jake find their seats, and Faith feels herself growing uncomfortable, but she doesn't know why. Jake can sense that something is wrong.

Jake quietly asks, "Faith, are you okay?"

"Not really. I have a very uneasy feeling about this trip."

"Is it about returning to Chicago and the memories waiting for you?"

"Yes, I think so. It's been a while. The memories aren't all good ones. I'm just not sure what the outcome is going to be, you know?"

"I know exactly what you mean. I felt the same way when I moved to Millstone from New York. It was hard, but Sam went with me, so I wasn't alone."

"Sam went with you? Wow, he wouldn't come with me, and I'm his best friend."

"Sam did want to come with you, but he's got a lot

on his plate right now. And he felt that since I went through what you are about to go through, that I would understand and help you better emotionally."

"Sam always knows what's best for me. Thank you again for coming with me."

"Absolutely no problem."

Faith begins to read a book she brought with her to pass the time while on the flight. Before long, she dozes off to sleep. Her mind takes her back to Chicago, to the hospital room, as she holds David's hand as he was dying of cancer. She recalls the last conversation she had with David before he closed his eyes forever, when he said, "I'm so sorry, Faith, that I didn't treat you and Cricket better. I stopped going with you both to the farm on holidays and even stopped going to church with you. I knew how important attending church was for you. You wanted Cricket to be raised in a Christian home. I blew that for you. I'm so sorry. I wasted so much time. Why did you stay with me all these years?"

"I made a vow, and I was honoring that vow. And Cricket is a Christian, David. She has faith, walks with God, and attends church regularly. At least we did that right. But none of that matters now, David. Just rest."

"It *does* matter, Faith. It's too late for me, but it's not too late for you. Get back to that part of your life. I know how important it was to you. And thank you."

"For what?"

"Leading me to Christ when we first started dating. I wish I had been better about my relationship with God. But I do know, when I die, I'll be in His kingdom. Thank you."

"You're welcome, David. Please, just rest."

Hours later, as she held his hand, he passed away peacefully.

The plane begins its descent, and Faith wakes up, realizing she fell asleep on Jake's shoulder.

"Oh, gosh, Jake, I'm so sorry. Why didn't you wake me?"

"I figured you needed the sleep, and I didn't mind, so I let you rest."

"Thank you. I guess I'm more tired than I realized."

Faith and Jake land in Chicago and hail a taxi to take them to the storage unit. Faith rents a truck, and they load her furniture and personal possessions on the vehicle.

"Look, Faith, I know you plan on hiring someone to drive this truck back to Millstone, but we can drive it back ourselves if you would like to do so."

"You're kidding, right?"

"No, I'm not kidding. It will save you some money, and if we trade off driving, we will only need to stop for food and gas. Come on, it will be an adventure."

"Gee, Jake, I'm not really the adventurous type anymore. Let me think about it for a moment." Faith pauses to mull over driving the truck back to Millstone, then says, "Hmm, well, it would save me money, and I would want all my things to reach Millstone in one piece. Hmm, any doubts about us doing this, speak now or forever hold your peace."

Jake said confidently, "I have no doubt at all.

Faith shrugs her shoulders, "Why not, ok, if you think we can do this, then, let's do it!"

Jake and Faith begin the journey back to Millstone. They make casual conversation for a few hours, then Faith falls asleep as Jake drives. Jake pulls into a service station for snacks and gas, and Faith drives for the next few hours while Jake sleeps. Faith realizes that she went to Chicago and left without having even one emotional incident. She begins to think about Millstone, and she broke into a grin. She knows now that Millstone is where she belongs.

Jake wakes up after a few hours and offers to drive, but Faith insists on continuing. Jake rubs the crick in his neck and says, "Whose idea was this again?"

Faith laughs. "Yours! Actually, the drive has been really relaxing. I'm enjoying it."

"Glad to hear that, Faith."

"So, Jake, do you miss missionary work?"

"Wow, that was a random question. Sometimes I do. I really loved traveling and meeting new people. Sometimes I even helped a few get to know the Lord. However, there is something to be said for settling down in one place out in the country. I really enjoy farming."

"I like it, too. You never thought about remarrying?"

"It crossed my mind a time or two."

"Do you ever get lonely?"

"Sometimes, but just because you are alone doesn't mean you get lonely. I have good friends, and I have God to lean on."

"You sound just like Sam."

"We are alike in some ways. It's really none of my business, but how is your relationship with God?"

"Nonexistent at the present time. But I promised Sam I would start praying again."

"May I ask why you feel it's nonexistent?"

"Honestly, I just drifted away from Him while my husband drifted away from our marriage. My husband didn't want to go to church with me or pray with me. I know it isn't an excuse, but that's what happened. Now I'm struggling to even talk to God. I think if my parents were still alive, things would be easier to get back in church and pray."

"Faith, you have good friends in Millstone."

"I know I do, and Sam has been trying to help me."

"Sometimes you just have to take that leap of faith and trust in God. Just because you left Him doesn't mean He ever left you. He's just waiting for you to talk to Him again."

"I know, Jake, I know."

"Are you ready for me to take the wheel and take us home?"

"We are about an hour from the next town, so we can switch off when we get there."

Jake and Faith continue to trade off driving until they reach Millstone. Sam is putting tools and roofing materials in his truck. He sees Faith and Jake drive through town towards Faith's farm. He smiles, knowing they made it home safely after the long drive.

Faith and Jake arrive at Faith's farm and begin unpacking boxes from the truck. Faith says, "We can unload the furniture in the morning if that's okay. I'm really tired, and I know you are as well. Wow, I hope this furniture fits in the house. I think it will if I give away my mom's sofa and loveseat."

"I'll take them. They will look great in my study! I'll drop by in the morning to help you unload the rest of the boxes and furniture from the truck. I can pick them up when we are finished."

"Great! Thank you again, Jake, for everything."

"I enjoyed it. See you tomorrow."

Jake leaves, and Faith drives to Bea's house to pick up Lily. Knocking on Bea's door, she says, "Bea, it's Faith."

"Just a minute!" Bea opens the door. "Well, you and Jake made good time. I didn't expect to see you until tomorrow morning."

"I know it's late. I hope it's okay. I should have

called first."

"Don't give it a second thought. Lily and I were watching a movie. It's not every day that I get to entertain someone from the city council."

"Good grief, Bea." As Faith walks into the living room, she sees Lily sitting on the sofa, eating a bowl of popcorn. Lily is wearing a baby blue nightcap. "What is that on her head, Bea?"

"Oh, that's Henry's old nightcap. I thought it would look cute on her," Bea says, smiling. "Well, we were about to finish the movie and head off to bed. I was afraid her little head would get cold."

Faith can't help but laugh at the nightcap, "Come on, Lily. Let's go home. Thank you again, Bea, for watching Lily for me."

"No problem at all. Any time you need to bring her over will be just fine with me. You know, since Henry passed away, it has been lonely out here. I enjoyed Lily's company."

Faith's heart and voice softened as she said, "How long has it been since Henry passed, Bea? Two years now?"

"Yes, two lonely years ago. You know, Henry and I met in the second grade. I fell off the monkey bars, and Henry helped me up. We were best friends from that moment on. Of course, as we got older, we fell madly in love. We never had an argument, and Henry never raised his voice at me. We had the perfect life. Then one day, he was gone. I still feel like a part of me is missing."

"I understand. Henry was a great man. I miss him, too."

"Well, I hate to keep you from getting home."

Faith wipes a tear from her eye, realizing how much Bea misses Henry. "So what movie were you watching?"

"Oklahoma, my favorite musical."

"I love that movie! Would you mind if we stayed and started it over?"

Bea's face lights up. "Not at all. And if it gets too late, you and Lily are welcome to stay in the guest room."

"That sounds like a plan, but we're going to need more popcorn."

Faith, Lily, and Bea watch the movie while reminiscing about old times. The next morning, Bea and Faith wake up early, eat breakfast, and then head off to work. Faith drives back to the farm to meet Jake to finish unloading the truck. Sam shows up to help, and in no time, it's all done, including loading Jake's truck with Faith's mom's sofa and loveseat.

Faith takes a small break, then begins her farm duties, and then the tedious task of making her childhood home her own. She decided to work while listening to music. She hadn't turned on her mom's radio since she came back to Milestone. She turned on the radio and walked away, excited to get busy. She was focused on packing away items and unpacking her things when she heard a familiar song on the radio, "I Can Only Imagine" by MercyMe. Her mother apparently had the radio tuned to a Christian radio station. There, on the radio, was her favorite song. She stopped working and sat down next to the radio. She listened intently as the song brought back memories of her church days. Tears started to stream down her cheeks. She felt sadness in her heart, something that she could not explain. There, next to the radio, was one of her mother's many Bibles. As she looked closer at it, she noticed a slip of paper placed between the pages. She slowly picked up the Bible and opened it to the page where the paper lay. She pulled out the slip of paper and saw that it was a prayer list that her mother had kept. There, at the top of the list, was Faith's name. Next to her name read, "Praying that Faith finds her way back to the Lord." Faith's heart sank when she realized that her mother had been praying for her and that she knew that Faith had lost her way. Anxiety began to fill her heart, and she called the one person who would understand: Sam. She phones him immediately.

"Hello?"

"Sam, it's me."

"What's wrong, Faith? I can tell you are crying."

"I was looking through Mom's Bible, and I found her prayer list. I was on top of her list! Did she ever mention to you about praying for me?"

"Yes, Faith. Sometimes she would pray alone, and sometimes she would pray with me. You know I was your parents' minister, right?"

"This is breaking my heart. My mom died knowing that I had lost my way. Why didn't you ever say anything to me? Why didn't she ever say anything to me?"

"Would you have listened?"

"If I had known I would lose her in a car accident, I would have listened to every word she said to me."

"But you didn't know that, did you?"

"No."

"Sometimes it is best to allow God to work in our lives while we remain still. Psalm 46:10 says, *'Be still and know that I am God.'* Your mom was doing just that, praying for you while remaining still. She believed in the power of prayer and allowing God to work in your life as well as her own life."

"I remember that scripture. It was … is … one of my favorites."

"Well, Faith, sometimes we need to be still so that God can work in our lives without our interference. Your mother knew that you were a Christian. Even though you have strayed away from Him, He has never left you. She knew with all her heart that you would find your way back to Him. In His time, not ours. God's timing is perfect, and your mother understood that about Him, Faith."

"I really don't understand, Sam. Please explain to me how God's timing is perfect."

"Okay, I'll try. Listen, God's timing is perfect at every stage of our lives. He teaches us what we need to know even as children, preparing to be adults. Little girls play with dolls, holding them, feeding them, changing their diapers, caring for them, and loving them. God plants this seed at an early age for little girls to understand how to nurture, care, and love so that one day, they will be good mothers. Little boys play in the dirt; they get scrappy and learn to hunt and fish. God plants this seed at an early age for boys to understand how to provide and protect so they can be good fathers. As our children get older, so do we; they become rebellious teenagers, breaking away from us, trying to find their feet. It's just part of God's perfect timing. I'm sure you remember those days. One day, our children are parents, and we become grandparents. Instead of us taking our children to the doctor, they drive us there. We don't hear our grown children call our name until the third or fourth time because we lose some of our hearing, and we use our cheater glasses more often to read the fine print until we realize it's regular print that we're trying to read. We don't spring out of bed; we slowly roll out. We find ourselves praying more often, talking to God like He's an old friend. As our bodies start to fail us, we get closer and closer to God. God's timing is perfect. We start to forget about the body that we have, and we start to think about the new body we get when we arrive in Heaven. When we realize that we can no longer take care of the ones we love and the things we love, we hand them over to God. We say, 'Lord, I trust you, take care of my family,' and we prepare to walk into His kingdom. God's timing is perfect. Psalms 27:14 says, '*Wait for the Lord; be strong and let your heart take courage; wait for the Lord.*' Your parents understood all about God's perfect timing. He perfectly times every stage of our life."

"Wow, Sam. You should use that in one of your sermons."

"I did. If you had come to church two Sundays ago, you would have heard it."

"Sorry, Sam."

"Your parents understood all about God's timing, Faith. Again, they knew that in His time, you would find your way back to Him."

"I guess I just drifted away, and staying away became a habit. I was afraid I had disappointed Him too much. I know it sounds like an excuse, but that fear was real."

"There is one phrase that is mentioned more than any other phrase in the Bible, and it is *fear not. Fear not* is written 365 times in the Bible. There's a 'fear not' for every day of the year. God tells us to not be afraid. He is always there for us, and He will always be waiting for us with open arms."

"Again, wow, Sam. You should definitely use that in a sermon."

"I did. If you had come to church four Sundays ago, you would have heard that, too."

"Touché, Sam. Point well taken." Faith remains silent for a few moments.

Sam feels that Faith needs to say something, but, not sure what it is, says, "You're quiet. I know something is on your mind. What is it?"

"I lost almost all feeling for David, Sam. There was no love left for him, but I didn't want him to die. If he had tried harder, maybe we could have gotten back to where we started. Maybe if I had prayed, things would have been different. Now it's too late. And maybe if I had prayed, I would still have my parents. Is God punishing me for not staying close to Him, for losing my faith?"

Sam is relieved that the actual issue with Faith's inability to talk to him is finally coming to light. "No, God isn't punishing you. He allows things to happen in our lives, but you are not being punished. We may never know the reason He allows our loved ones to leave this earth, especially when they pass away suddenly. Like I said before, He has a plan for all of us. We aren't all meant to live to be a hundred years old. I like to think that He needs us with Him sooner than we think; that our leaving this earth is for a reason more for His purpose than not. I know it's hard to understand, but He is always working in our lives. He brings people into our lives for a reason and out of our lives for a specific purpose. We won't know that purpose until we get to Heaven to be with Him for eternity. Then and only then will we know in heaven what we always wondered here on earth. What I do know is that the closer you get to Him, the more you will understand that we are not meant to know everything while we are here. That's where faith comes into play. The closer you walk with Him, the less pain you will feel and the more you will begin to understand His plan for you. Start reading His word again, Faith. Everything we need to know, for now, is all in there."

"Thank you, Sam. I'll be in church this Sunday and every Sunday to come."

"Glad to hear it, Faith. Do you feel better now?"

"Yes, a little better. You've always been there for me, Sam."

"Always, Faith. By the way, your mom named you Faith because her faith in God was absolute."

"She told me that once. I understand it now. I miss them both every day."

"I miss them as well. They loved you and Ben more than you could ever know, but they are home now."

"I know. It's still just very difficult, but I know they are in Heaven, the Lord's Kingdom."

"Yes, they are, Faith. I can just see your mom listening to Mary, Jesus' mother, telling everyone what it was like to raise the Son of God. And hearing Sarah talk about becoming a mother at ninety years old. Your mom will be drawn to amazing women like Esther and Ruth, because she was an amazing woman as well. Your dad will be mesmerized listening to Moses as he tells the story of parting the Red Sea and listening to Joshua as he tells how he felt leading the Israelites across the River Jordan over to the Promised Land without Moses."

"I never thought of heaven like that, Sam. To be able to see Jesus and all the people we have read about in the Bible would be absolutely indescribable."

"It will be amazing, Faith. Your parents and David are there, experiencing all the wonderful things Jesus promised us."

Both Sam and Faith sat for a moment thinking about Heaven and what it will be like for them someday when they enter God's Kingdom. The room went utterly silent, and then, as if Sam popped out of a deep trance, he lively said, "Dinner at Dad's tonight?"

"Sure, I would love to see your dad."

"I'll see you at seven."

Chapter 9

$\mathcal{F}$aith continues to set up the house, then gets ready to go to dinner with Sam and his father. She decides to put Lily in a large, emerald green tea garden hat. Faith arrives at Mr. Wright's house and knocks twice on the front door. Sam hears the knocks and heads to the front door while hollering, "Come on in, ladies." Sam is delighted when he sees Lily in her huge emerald green hat. "Well, Lily, you look absolutely fetching in that exceptionally large green hat. Faith, where on earth did you get that hat?"

Faith and Lily enter the house. "It was Mom's hat. I

found it in the closet as I was clearing out a few things. She always wanted to go to the Kentucky Derby, so she bought this hat just in case. You know how much she loved Secretariat."

Mr. Wright chimes in. "Oh, I know. That was a great horse. There will be another one like him. I find it hard to believe that your mom would want to go to a horse track, Faith."

"Not to bet money, Mr. Wright; just to see the horses run and for her to wear that crazy hat."

Sam walks into the dining room carrying a platter. "Dinner is ready. Let's eat."

Faith, Sam, and Mr. Wright all sit down at the table. Lily tries to jump up in a chair, but her hat is too big, so Faith removes it temporarily. Lily finally jumps up in her seat at the table. Sam says grace, and everyone begins to eat.

As Mr. Wright passes the dinner rolls, he says, "Faith, I love it when you and Lily join us for dinner. It makes the house seem warm when people are filled in it."

"Is it me or Lily that you love to see? Seems Bea enjoys her company, too."

"Well, she is a special little dog. Your mom spoiled her like she was one of her own children."

"Don't I know it. I still don't understand why Mom put hats on this dog."

Mr. Wright smiles directly at Faith. "Because she

missed putting hats on you."

Faith is taken aback by Mr. Wright's comment, slowly uttering, "What?"

"I remember when you were about three or four years old; your mother had a hat for you every day of the week. Don't you remember?"

Faith starts to recall the memory, "I *do* remember wearing hats all the time when I was a kid! Wow, I had forgotten that."

Sam looks at Lily. "But I have to say, Lily wears them better."

Faith squints her eyes at Sam as she puts a spoonful of mashed potatoes in her mouth. For the next hour, Mr. Wright recalls various childhood stories about Sam and Faith getting into mischief, and about Faith's parents and Sam's mom. The stories brought tender and joyful moments. After dinner, Sam and Faith help with the dishes, and Mr. Wright heads off to bed. Sam walks into the study and tells Faith, "I'm going to work on the puzzle. Care to join me?"

"Sure." Faith sees that the puzzle hasn't been touched since the last time she was over for dinner. "Gee, Sam, it looks like you haven't touched this thing in weeks."

"Well, I kind of thought you might work on it a little here and there while you were checking on Dad."

"Sorry, Sam. I come by to check on your day every few days like you asked, but I never come in this room."

"Oh, it's fine. Sit. Work."

Faith begins to pick up the puzzle pieces that complete the frame. She puts the last straight edge piece in place and says excitedly, "There, the frame is finished!" Faith stares at the frame, trying to see a glimpse of a picture. "I still have no idea what this picture could be, Sam. Who buys a puzzle not knowing what they are putting together?"

Sam said with a smirk, "I do."

Sam and Faith focus on quietly working on the puzzle for a while. Faith recalls the conversation she had with Sam earlier and says, "I have thought about everything you said earlier on the phone."

"And?"

"You were right about everything. I know when and where I started to fade away from my faith, but honestly, it was so gradual I didn't really see how far away I became from God."

"It doesn't matter. What matters is where you are today, now, here in this room, realizing that you need God in your life. I'm not saying that it's going to be easy. I'm saying that you are on the right path, day by day, moment by moment. Start talking to God, building a relationship with Him. Pray, be still, and watch the amazing things He can do with your life."

"When I left for college, I thought I had my entire life figured out. I planned on getting my Agricultural

Science degree and then coming back to the farm and running it for my parents. They made it clear to us that when they passed, I would inherit the farm, and Ben would inherit the lake cabin acreage. Of course, I finished my degree, but David proposed, and that was that. We moved to Chicago."

"Faith, are you happy back here in Millstone?"

"Of course I am. I love it here and always have. Even when David wouldn't come with me to visit, I still brought Cricket for every holiday and several weeks during the summer. I really didn't want to go back to Chicago; I wanted to stay here at home."

"But Chicago was your home, right?"

"Technically, yes, but in my heart, I always considered the family farm as my home."

"Like I said, God knows your heart, and He knows it has always belonged here in Millstone. Maybe His plan for you was to return home one day to help the local farmers. Millstone is a huge farming town, and the farmers have had their ups and downs. Your education could benefit our farming community immensely. Remember, God's timing is perfect. Maybe God didn't want you to come back here after college. Maybe His plan was for you to stay in Chicago and start a family. Maybe you were meant to meet David to lead him to Christ because you were the only one who could have reached him."

"Maybe you're right, Sam."

"Maybe I am, and maybe I'm just guessing. What I know for sure is that if you allow Him to work in your life, He will."

"Thank you, Sam. You have a way of making me feel better and not such a failure in life."

"I'm always here if you need me. And you are not a failure in life. Life happens to everyone, and sometimes we just need to get back on the path He wants us to travel."

Faith begins to think about her parents, especially her mom, and the prayer list she found. She thinks about Sam's mom and asks, "Do you still miss your mom?"

"Every day. But it doesn't hurt every day like it did when we first lost her. Time will pass, Faith, and instead of pain consuming your heart, it will be filled with sweet memories. Instead of tears of sorrow, they will be tears of laughter, remembering all the wonderful times you shared with them both."

"I still can't believe they are gone. I think things would be easier if my brother were here and not in Rome."

"He is handling the loss in his own way, Faith. He found someone to fill the emptiness he feels in his heart."

"Oh, is that it? Is that what he's doing?"

Sam chuckles. "Yes, I believe that is what he is doing, Faith. Now back to this puzzle."

"Oh, by the way, I have all the animals ready for the petting zoo for the Fall Festival next month."

"That's great, and I just about got the roof completed."

"Well, that's the best news I've heard all day. I get so worried about you when you get on that rooftop. I really wish you would hire a professional to finish it."

"Yes, you keep telling me that, so I'll stop mentioning it to you."

"I'm going to worry whether we discuss it or not. Okay, I need to get Lily home because it is way past her bedtime. She has a council meeting at eight sharp in the morning. See you tomorrow."

"You bet. Be careful."

The next morning, Faith wakes up and gets Lily ready for the town council meeting. As she is about to walk out the door, her cell phone rings.

"Hello?"

"Faith, it's Bea. There was an accident. It's Sam."

"What? What happened to Sam?"

"It seems that he wanted to get an early start on the church roof, so he was up there at dawn. The roof was wet from the morning dew, and he slipped off the roof and fell. They rushed him to the hospital. It just happened. I'm heading to the hospital now, but I wanted to call you first and let you know."

"What about his dad? Has anyone called him yet?"

"He was helping out at the church, so he was there when it happened. He was in the ambulance when the EMTs drove Sam to the emergency room."

"I'm on my way."

Faith leaves Lily at home and drives urgently to the emergency room. When she arrives, Mr. Wright is sitting in the emergency waiting area.

"Mr. Wright, how is he? What's going on? Is he okay?"

"We don't know anything yet. It might be a bad concussion or skull fracture. We will know more after they finish running tests and scans."

Over the next few hours, several people arrived at the emergency room to support Sam. Mr. Wright encouraged them to go home and rest. He promised them that any news would be relayed to them. The only people left at the hospital were Faith, Mr. Wright, Bea, and Jake.

"We've been waiting here for hours and haven't heard one word about Sam's condition," Faith says.

"The best thing we can do for Sam is pray," Mr. Wright replied.

The emergency room doctor came out to speak to Sam's father. "Mr. Wright?"

"Randy—I mean Doctor Simmons. How is he, Doc?"

"You can call me Randy, Mr. Wright. Well, Sam has what we call a basilar skull fracture. When Sam fell, he fractured his skull, and the fracture injured the blood vessels that supply the brain. I know this is hard to hear, but it can cause permanent brain damage or even death. We are going to watch him for the next 24 to 48 hours. I have called a specialist from Houston to look at his case. I have already sent him the information so he can help us figure out our next course of action. I'm waiting for his call. It will take him some time to look over all his tests, X-rays, and scans, so be patient. Easier said than done, I know, but Sam is strong and in exceptionally good shape. Sam is sedated and in no pain. As soon as I find out something, I will call you. Sam needs to rest. I will have nurses monitoring him constantly."

Mr. Wright anxiously asks, "Can I sit with him?"

"He is in critical care and in a very fragile state, Mr. Wright. He really needs to rest. There is nothing you can do here for Sam. Please go home, get some rest, and try to be patient. I will call you as soon as I hear from the specialist."

"Okay. Thank you, Randy. I know Sam is in good hands. But I really don't want to go home. My boy is fighting for his life, so I should be here, but I know there is nothing I can do for him but pray."

"Let me drive you home, Mr. Wright," Faith says. "I'll come back and stay in the ER so that you can go home and rest."

"You need to go home and rest as well, Faith. My

truck is at the church. Can you drive me there?"

"Of course."

Faith drives Mr. Wright to the church. Instead of getting in his truck to go home, he goes inside to pray. Faith's eyes begin to fill with tears as she thinks of the possibility of losing Sam and how it would affect his dad, his friends, the church, and especially, Faith herself. She begins the drive home, and a sense of fear and anxiety comes over her. First, she loses David, then her parents, and now possibly Sam. She reaches her home, runs inside, and falls to her knees to pray. "Lord, forgive me of my sins and purify my heart. I'm so sorry that I walked away from you. I'm sorry I allowed my heart to harden. I'm sorry that I didn't lean on you when I lost David and my parents. I'm leaning on you now and trusting you to heal Sam. He trusts you, too. I'm sorry that I have forgotten how to pray to you. But I know in my heart that you are almighty and that you know me better than I know myself. Give Sam strength. Comfort his father and his friends. Put a peace in their hearts that you have Sam and you are working on healing him at this very moment. Amen."

Faith was worried about Mr. Wright, so she got in her truck and drove to his house to check on him. She knocks and he answers the door.

"I hope I'm not intruding, but I wanted to check on you."

"I'm doing okay. Come on in, Faith. I've been want-ing to go to the hospital, but the doc wants Sam to rest. I'm trusting God to help the doc make good decisions for Sam. I'm just waiting for him to call me."

"I know. Do you mind if I wait here also?"

"Not at all. I don't want to be alone right now. Hey, let's you and I work on Sam's puzzle to pass the time until Doc calls us."

"Sure. Sounds good."

Faith and Mr. Wright work on the puzzle, trying to remain patient while they wait for the doctor to provide an update about Sam. A few hours pass, and, without realizing it, the puzzle is only missing two pieces to be put in place. Mr. Wright and Faith had been talking about times gone by and hadn't paid any attention to the puzzle picture. Faith puts the last two pieces in place and looks at the picture. Tears fill her eyes as she recognizes the picture of the puzzle. It is a picture of Faith and Sam kneeling at the cross at church camp when they were kids.

Mr. Wright realizes Faith recognizes the picture and says, "Sam found that picture of you two and had it turned into a puzzle."

"You knew?"

"Of course, I knew. I know everything that goes on in this town."

"Why did Sam do it?"

"Well, you know Sam. He never really comes out

and says things; he finds other ways to get his meaning across. Ways that may start a spark in someone's heart. He's been praying for you for a long time. He wanted you to remember that day. You told him it was the best and most important day of your life."

"I remember it like it was yesterday. Wow, my mom, Sam; anyone else praying for me?"

"Anyone who cares about you has probably been down on their knees a time or two. You've been through a lot, Faith. Losing David and then both your parents. That's tough to get through all alone. You haven't really let anyone in to help comfort you."

"I know, I know. And now Sam."

"Sam will pull through this; I know. He has too much to do, and he's tough. Don't you worry about him. But you can pray for him. He's in God's hands now. And I know God will take care of him. If we hand our worries over to God, and then still worry, we aren't really handing our worries over to Him, right? We have to trust Him and have faith."

Faith replies, "I agree and understand what you are saying, but having faith is still really hard for me to grasp."

Mr. Wright sat for a moment before replying. "Faith, do you remember Rowdy, the Louisiana Catahoula Leopard dog we had when you and Sam were kids?"

"Yes, I do. That dog was very protective and very smart."

"Rowdy would never let anything or anyone come through the gate entrance, nor would he let anyone in the house. If he didn't know who you were, you were not allowed on the property. If Sam were outside playing, Rowdy would be right by his side. When we went to sleep every night, we slept with no worries because we knew Rowdy was in control and would protect us. We trusted him so much that we never even locked our doors at night. I trusted him with our lives. Before I went into the house for the night, I would tell Rowdy goodnight, take care of my family, and we love you. That's faith in a nutshell. Handing your life over to God, never to worry about anything because He will take care of any issue or concern. I give Him full control of my life, and I know, without a doubt, the decisions He makes for me are always the right ones."

Faith nods her head. "I actually understand now. Thank you."

"You're very welcome."

Mr. Wright fell asleep in his recliner, and Faith fell asleep on the sofa. An hour later, the phone rings, and Mr. Wright and Faith spring to their feet. Mr. Wright answers the phone.

"Hello? Yes. Yes. I'm on my way."

"Was it the hospital?"

"Yes. It was Dr. Simmons. Sam does have a skull fracture just as he predicted. He said that Sam is still unconscious, but I would be able to see him for a few moments. Dr. Simmons is waiting for the specialist from Houston to arrive shortly to discuss our next step."

"I'll drive!"

Mr. Wright and Faith arrive at the hospital. Mr. Wright goes in to see Sam. Faith watches through the window to Sam's room. Mr. Wright sits next to Sam's bed, holds his hand, and begins talking to him. Sam doesn't respond, and Mr. Wright begins to pray. He kisses Sam on the forehead and leaves the room.

Mr. Wright returns to the waiting room with Faith. Bea and Jake arrive for support just as Dr. Simmons enters the waiting area.

"Mr. Wright, the specialist from Houston, should be arriving soon. He has a plan for Sam. It would be a good idea for you to go see Sam again before we start with the preparations. We will explain everything in my office."

Mr. Wright goes into the room to see Sam again. He holds Sam's hand as he kneels down by his bed to pray. He gets up, kisses Sam on the forehead again, and whispers that he loves him in his ear. Dr. Simmons is waiting outside the room to escort Mr. Wright to his office, where he will meet the specialist.

Faith, Jake, and Bea sit in silence for a few minutes, not really knowing what to say.

Faith breaks the silence with a story about Sam. "When Sam and I were kids, if something was upsetting us, we would get the Bible, close our eyes, open it, and put our finger directly on the page. Then we would open our eyes to see the scripture that was under our fingers. Believe it or not, every time, the scripture would be something that we needed to hear. It was always something that spoke to us that helped with the problem in our lives."

Jake looks at Faith and says, "I have my Bible in the truck. I'll go get it." And with that, he leaped up and hurried to his truck to retrieve his Bible.

As Bea and Faith watch him leave the ER, Bea looks at Faith. "We need all the help we can get, hun. Open that Bible and see what God needs us to hear."

Jake returns with his Bible. The cover is worn, and there are Post-it notes on several pages. Jake sits down, looks at his Bible, and says, "This is my first and only Bible. I've taken it all over the world." Jake closes his eyes, opens the Bible, and puts his finger on one of the pages. He opens his eyes to the scripture under his finger, Proverbs 3:5, and reads it aloud, "*Trust in the Lord with all your heart and do not lean on your own understanding.* Wow, right on target with my feelings. I don't understand the science of what is happening to Sam, but I don't need to understand it because God does. He created every ounce of us and knows how to heal our bodies and our minds. So we don't need to put our faith and trust in anything or anyone but Him."

As Jake hands his Bible to Bea, he says, "Your turn, Bea."

Bea does the same thing as Jake: closes her eyes, opens the Bible, and places her finger on a scripture. She opens her eyes and reads aloud, "Second Corinthians 5:7, *for we walk by faith, not by sight.* The situation we are in with Sam does require us to trust and have faith. We cannot see what we see, for we see someone we love who is physically broken and in a fragile state. We must trust what we know, and that is God is in control of everything, everywhere, and can heal and mend a body He created."

Bea, with tears in her eyes, passes Jake's Bible to Faith, who repeats Bea and Jake's action. She opens her eyes and reads the scripture beneath her finger. "Psalms 46:10, *Be still and know that I am God."* Faith pauses for a moment before she softly says, "Sam and I recently discussed this scripture. Sam reminded me to trust God and surrender all my worries to Him, for God is in control of every situation, every circumstance, because God is all-mighty and all-powerful. We need to do exactly that and hand Sam over to God."

Faith, Jake, and Bea bow their heads as Faith begins to pray aloud. "Lord, our God and heavenly father, thank you for Sam and thank you for speaking to us through your word. We trust you, and we know Sam is in your hands, for there is no better place for him to be,

Lord. Please heal him, for we know you are all-powerful and all-mighty; nothing is impossible for you. Thank you for your son, Jesus Christ, for we find hope in the resurrection and that in Him, death is defeated. Help us keep our eyes fixed on you always, Lord. For we ask these things in your most precious name, Jesus Christ our Lord and Savior. Amen."

"Amen," came from Mr. Wright as he stood in the doorway listening to the prayer. Mr. Wright walks up to Faith and takes her hands. He can see her eyes are filling up with tears. He pats her on the shoulder and says, "You go see Sam. I know you need to see him, and Sam needs to know you are here, too."

Faith hugs Mr. Wright and then heads toward the intensive care section. Mr. Wright stands by the room observation window, silently praying. Faith sits beside Sam and holds his hand. She leans in close to Sam's ear and says, "You were right, Sam. You were right about everything. I've been praying for you. You're my best friend, and I love you, and you can't leave us now. Everyone in this town depends on you, so you can't leave them just yet either. I pray that God's plan for you is to stay here with all of us. God is in control, Sam." Tears silently roll down Faith's cheek. "I finished the puzzle, Sam. It was the sweetest thing anyone has ever done for me. Thank you. I remember that amazing day, and I got the message loud and clear. I'm praying again."

With his eyes still closed, Sam whispers, "I had to fall off a roof to get you to work on that puzzle?"

Faith's eyes widen as she looks at Sam. She looks at Mr. Wright through the room window and waves for him to come in. Mr. Wright rushes in. "He's awake! Sam's talking!"

Mr. Wright rushes into the room. "I knew it. I knew God would pull you out of this. Faith, will you find the nursing staff and tell them Sam's awake?"

"Of course."

Faith heads for the door and stops to turn around to look at Sam. Sam opens his eyes, sees her, and smiles. Faith rushes to get a nurse. They all stand around in amazement at Sam's miraculous recovery. Dr. Simmons rushes into the room and says, "He's awake? I can't believe it!"

Mr. Wright, still holding Sam's hand, turns to Dr. Simmons. "*With God, all things are possible.* Matthew 19:26." Mr. Wright looks at Faith. "That is the scripture I put my finger on, and I know it to be true."

Faith nods her head in agreement.

Dr. Simmons, still in amazement, says, "I believe it! We need to run more tests and scans. I'm amazed. I can say that I've actually witnessed a miracle."

Faith reaches for Sam's other hand. "I've witnessed a miracle, too."

Chapter 10

As the days passed, Sam continued to make an amazing recovery. Mr. Wright, Faith, Bea, and Jake would take turns staying with Sam at the hospital during therapy sessions, meals, and even while he slept. Sam had always been there for each one of them, and now, it was their turn to be there for him. And of course, he talked about God and how blessed he was to walk with Him, even as he lay in a hospital bed.

Faith took the puzzle Sam had made for her, glued the back, and placed it in a frame. It was her most prized possession. She hung it in a place where she could see it as she walked into her home. She wanted to be reminded of that day, every day, as she and Sam kneeled before the cross at church camp. She found herself praying more and more each day, and reading scripture became a habit. Every morning before Faith got out of bed, she prayed. She asked God to guide her life every moment of the day, to open doors that He wanted her to walk through, and to put His plan for her in motion. She wanted her life to glorify Him, and she wanted people to see Him shine through her at every stage of her life.

***

A month later, Faith is pushing Sam in a wheelchair on the fairgrounds at the Fall Festival. Mr. Wright is walking beside Sam, pulling Lily in a wagon with a halo of daisies on her head.

Sam looks around at the grounds. "Wow, everything looks great. You all did such an amazing job pulling this all together."

Faith replies, "Well, the entire town pitched in and made it happen. They wanted to make you proud."

"Mission accomplished. Hey, is that the mayor in the dunking booth? Take me over there. I'd love to dunk him."

"Sam, the doctor said to take it easy," Mr. Wright reminded him. "Even though he said he witnessed a miracle, your skull is still healing. You will be back to your old self soon, so don't rush it."

"Yes, you're right, Dad, let's not push it. There's always next year."

Faith had forgotten how wonderful the Fall Festival was and became distracted by all the wonders and colors of the season. She loved seeing the people of Millstone happy and laughing. As she gets lost in the moment, she feels someone touch her shoulder. As she turns to see who it is, she sees Bea wearing a floppy gardening hat covered with fall leaves and tiny pumpkins.

Faith's lips curl in amusement. "I guess Lily isn't the only one who has a sense of class and style."

"Why should she have all the fun?" Bea chortles. "I made it myself. I wanted to feel festive today."

"Well, you achieved that particular goal. You look great, Bea. As a matter of fact, I've seen several people wearing unusual hats today. What's up with that?"

"Well, we wanted to surprise you! In honor of your mother and Lily, we are having a festive homemade hat contest this afternoon. The winner will get two gift certificates at Nolan's Restaurant. And Nolan, Sam, Lily, and you are going to be the judges."

"Oh, Bea, that's a wonderful idea. Mom would love it! Thank you for thinking about her and honoring her with this contest."

"Your mom was a huge part of this town and this festival. Your parents always worked so hard to make each Fall festival a huge success. We are happy to do it."

Faith's eyes begin to tear as she remembers her parents and the way the town is honoring them.

As Faith wipes away her tears, she notices someone approaching Bea from behind. As the person gets closer, she realizes it is Sandra Simmons, the woman who scolded Bea for reading her letter from her sister. Faith's expression unconsciously turns to slight fear as Sandra pats Bea on the shoulder.

Bea turns around and faces Sandra. "Hello, Mrs. Simmons. Can I help you?"

Sandra replies brightly. "Yes, as a matter of fact, you can, Bea. Randy and I are going on vacation to Ireland, and I would really hate to miss one of my sister's weekly letters. I was wondering, when the letter arrives, would you possibly phone me and read the letter to me? It would mean so much if you would do that, and I hope it won't be an imposition."

Bea's face lit up with delight. "Oh, Mrs. Simmons, it would be no imposition at all. I would be glad to help out in any way possible."

Sandra nods her head in affirmation. "You have my number. And please, Bea, call me Sandra." Sandra looks cheerily at Sam, Mr. Wright, and Faith before turning to join Randy at the concession booth.

Faith raises her eyebrows. "The Lord works in mysterious ways."

Bea, Sam, and Mr Wright simultaneously nod their heads in agreement, still a little shocked by what they just witnessed.

Then, Faith stands still as she hears familiar music. She looks up at the stage to see Hanson performing "MMMBop." Faith looks at Sam. "Oh my gosh! Sam, did you do this?"

"Nope, not me." Sam nods his head towards Jake, who is walking towards them. Jake has a short haircut and a clean-shaven face. Faith is shocked by how great Jake looks, and she catches herself staring at him. She sees his handsome features and the deep dimples on each side of his face when he smiles. For the first time in her life, she experiences what some people would call 'butterflies' in her stomach. Faith is at a loss for words, which has never happened to her before, as she looks at his soft eyes that seem much bluer than she remembered.

Faith snaps herself back to reality and realizes that Jake must have had something to do with this. "Jake? Did you do this?"

"I made a call to someone who I thought would be able to get them here to perform." Jake looks past Faith at someone standing behind her. It is her daughter, Cricket.

Faith sees her daughter, and joy overfills her heart as she hugs Cricket tightly. "Cricket! You're here! I've missed you so much."

"I've missed you, too, Mom. And I pulled some strings to get Hanson here because I know they are Lily's favorite group."

Faith looks at Jake with appreciation and adoration. She gives him a big hug. "Thank you, Jake."

Jake, still hugging Faith, beams. "My pleasure."

Faith now knows in her heart that if God opens a door for her, she will trust Him completely and walk through it. She closes her eyes and silently prays, "Okay, Lord, I see the door and I'm taking my first step through it." Faith beams at Jake, grabs his hand, and says, "Come on!" as she leads him towards the edge of the stage. Mr. Wright, Sam, Bea, and Cricket quickly follow behind them as they sense something surprising is happening. As Faith listens to the music, she looks around the fairgrounds. Everyone she loves is right there, right now, and she looks towards the heavens and thanks God for all the blessings she has received in her life. She also knows that her faith will grow each day and she will continue to walk with God for the rest of her days, never to wander away from Him again.

www.ingramcontent.com/pod-product-compliance
Lightning Source LLC
Chambersburg PA
CBHW030819200726
48288CB00004B/1302